THE BOXCAR CHILDREN®

THE WOODSHED MYSTERY

Time to Read® is an early reader program designed to guide children to literacy success regardless of age or grade level. The program's three levels correspond to stages of reading readiness, making book selection straightforward, and assuring that when it's time for a child to read, the right book is waiting.

— Level 1 —
Beginning to Read
- Large, simple type
- Basic vocabulary
- Word repetition
- Strong illustration support

— Level 2 —
Reading with Help
- Short sentences
- Engaging stories
- Simple dialogue
- Illustration support

— Level 3 —
Reading Independently
- Longer sentences
- Harder words
- Short paragraphs
- Increased story complexity

Library of Congress Cataloging-in-Publication data is on file with the publisher.

Copyright © 2020 by Albert Whitman & Company
Hardcover edition first published in the United States of America
in 2020 by Albert Whitman & Company
Paperback edition first published in the United States of America
in 2020 by Albert Whitman & Company
ISBN 978-0-8075-9216-8 (paperback)
ISBN 978-0-8075-9211-3 (ebook)

TIME TO READ® is a registered trademark
of Albert Whitman & Company.

THE BOXCAR CHILDREN® is a registered trademark
of Albert Whitman & Company.

Printed in China
10 9 8 7 6 5 4 3 2 1 T&N 24 23 22 21 20

Cover and interior art by Shane Clester

Visit the Boxcar Children online at www.boxcarchildren.com.
For more information about Albert Whitman & Company,
visit our website at www.albertwhitman.com.

THE BOXCAR CHILDREN®

THE WOODSHED MYSTERY

Based on the book by
Gertrude Chandler Warner

Albert Whitman & Company
Chicago, Illinois

One morning, Grandfather
had big news.
Great Aunt Jane was moving!
Benny did not understand.
"Moving?" he said.
"Moving is not big news. See?"
Benny ran in a circle.
Grandfather smiled.
"This is a big move, Benny.
My sister is coming to live in
the house where we grew up.
We are all going to go help!"

Henry, Jessie, Violet, and
Benny Alden had not always
lived with Grandfather.
After their parents died,
the children had run away.
For a little while, they had lived
in a boxcar in the woods.

Then Grandfather found them.
He gave them a real home.
He even brought the boxcar!

"There is the Bean farm!"
said Grandfather.
"As kids, Andy Bean was our
best friend.
Jane was very sad when he
moved away."
The Aldens were going to stay
with Andy's brother.
Aunt Jane's house was
next door.
It needed to be fixed up.

"Do you grow beans?"
Benny asked Mr. Bean.
Benny liked to eat,
and he loved beans.
Mr. Bean shook his head.
"We raise chickens."
Benny frowned.
"They give us lots of these,"
said Mr. Bean.
Benny cheered up.
He liked eggs almost as much
as he liked beans.
While the children ate breakfast,
Grandfather and Mr. Bean
made plans.

"A lot has changed over the years," said Grandfather.
"The house looks very old."
Benny thought it looked scary.
"Don't worry, Benny,"
said Jessie.
"It won't look so strange once we fix it up.
Though, it will take a lot of work..."

Beep! Beep!

Honk!

"We will have a lot of help," said Grandfather.

"Grandfather!" said Henry.

"How did you find so many helpers?"

Grandfather smiled.

"Some things do not change. News still travels fast in this town."

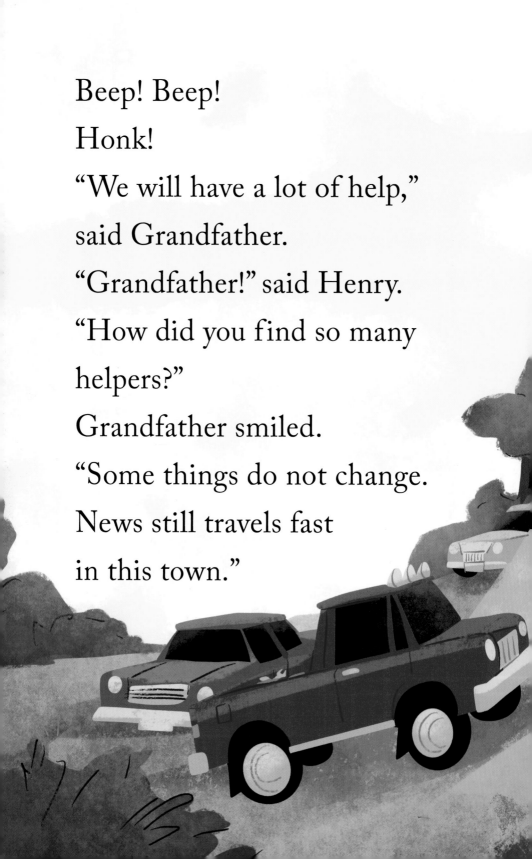

Day after day, the Aldens
worked on the house.
Little by little, the house did
not seem so strange.

Then one day, something strange did happen…

"Eggs are missing from
the coop!"
Mr. Bean scratched his head.
Everyone looked at Benny.
They all knew how much
he liked to eat.
"I would not take food,"
said Benny, "not even beans!"
If Benny had not taken the
eggs, where had they gone?

Soon Aunt Jane's house
was ready.
The children went exploring.
They found a little building.
It was just as old as the house.
To Benny, it was just as scary.
"Don't worry, Benny,"
said Henry.
"It's only a woodshed."

But it was more than that…

Inside, there was a bed of hay,
a stool, a table,
a spoon, and a dish.
On the dish were three eggs!
Was there a person staying
in the woodshed?

The children ran to tell
Grandfather what they
had found.
When they came back, they
found something even stranger.
The bed of hay was gone.
There was no stool or table.
No dish or spoon, and no eggs!

"There's a mystery here!"
said Benny.

The next day, Aunt Jane
arrived.
The children did not tell her
about their mystery in the
woodshed.
They did not want
to worry her.
They did show her all of their
hard work.
"It's wonderful!" said Aunt Jane.
"Now, I have something
to show you."

"This house is very old,"
Aunt Jane said.
"It was built many,
many years ago.
At the time, our country was
still fighting to be free.
People hid here to stay safe."

With that, Aunt Jane opened
a secret door!

"Did you hide here?"
asked Benny.
Aunt Jane laughed.
"I am not that old.
Your grandfather, Andy Bean,
and I used to play in this room."
Aunt Jane sighed.
"We had such great adventures."
The children looked
at each other.
Did Aunt Jane miss
Andy Bean?

That night, the Aldens asked Mr. Bean about his brother. "Andy loved adventures," said Mr. Bean.

"One day he went on an adventure and did not return."

"Are you sad he did not say good-bye?" asked Violet.

Mr. Bean shook his head. "I just hope he is okay."

The next day, the children got
back to their mystery.
Where had everything in the
woodshed gone?
Violet had an idea.
She knew the woodshed was
just as old as the house.
If there was a secret room
in the house, maybe…

there was one in the woodshed!

The secret room had many
old treasures.
It also had a bed of hay,
a stool, a table,
and an egg on a dish!
Someone was living in the
woodshed!
After the children stopped by,
the person had moved their
things out of sight!
Who was it?

The Aldens were about
to find out.

"Andy Bean!" said Jessie.

The man nodded.

Then he explained.

He had come to see Aunt Jane.

After all these years,

he missed her.

"How did you know she was

moving here?" asked Jessie.

Andy smiled.

"News still travels fast

in this town."

"Why aren't you staying with your brother?" asked Henry.

Andy sighed.

"I was afraid he would be upset," said Andy.

"I moved away so quickly, all those years ago."

"Mr. Bean isn't upset," said Violet.

"And guess what?" said Benny.

"We think Aunt Jane misses you too!"

Back at the house, they got
their answer.
Aunt Jane gave Andy Bean
a big hug.
So did Mr. Bean.
Grandfather had been right
all along.
Many things had changed over
the years...

But there were still some things
that stayed the same.

Keep reading with the Boxcar Children!

Henry, Jessie, Violet, and Benny used to live in a Boxcar. Now they have adventures everywhere they go! Adapted from the beloved chapter book series, these early readers allow kids to begin reading with the stories that started it all.

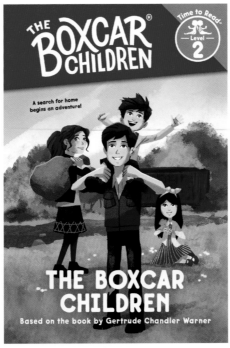

HC 978-0-8075-0839-8 · US $12.99
PB 978-0-8075-0835-0 · US $3.99

SURPRISE ISLAND

Based on the movie *Surprise Island*
Based on the book by Gertrude Chandler Warner

HC 978-0-8075-7675-5 · US $12.99
PB 978-0-8075-7679-3 · US $3.99

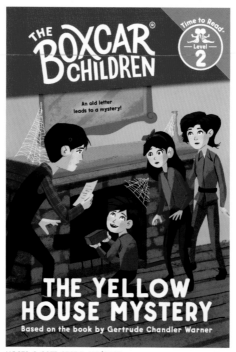

THE YELLOW
HOUSE MYSTERY

Based on the book by Gertrude Chandler Warner

HC 978-0-8075-9367-7 · US $12.99
PB 978-0-8075-9370-7 · US $3.99

MYSTERY RANCH

HC 978-0-8075-5402-9 · US $12.99
PB 978-0-8075-5435-7 · US $3.99

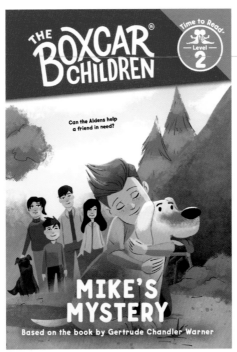

MIKE'S MYSTERY

HC 978-0-8075-5142-4 · US $12.99
PB 978-0-8075-5139-4 · US $3.99

GERTRUDE CHANDLER WARNER discovered when she was teaching that many readers who like an exciting story could find no books that were both easy and fun to read. She decided to try to meet this need, and her first book, *The Boxcar Children*, quickly proved she had succeeded.

Miss Warner drew on her own experiences to write the mystery. As a child she spent hours watching trains go by on the tracks opposite her family home. She often dreamed about what it would be like to set up housekeeping in a caboose or freight car—the situation the Alden children find themselves in.

While the mystery element is central to each of Miss Warner's books, she never thought of them as strictly juvenile mysteries. She liked to stress the Aldens' independence and resourcefulness and their solid New England devotion to using up and making do. The Aldens go about most of their adventures with as little adult supervision as possible—something else that delights young readers.

Miss Warner lived in Putnam, Connecticut, until her death in 1979. During her lifetime, she received hundreds of letters from girls and boys telling her how much they liked her books.